To Reb

from Michael

xxoo

Fairy stories hold a fascination for children that cannot be equalled. This story has been adapted for beginner readers but if your child is not able to read, you can read this delightful story aloud. For your child, listening to a story in a relaxed atmosphere is a vital part of the learning process. For you, the reader, there is the opportunity to discuss the feelings the story conjures up and the meanings of any unfamiliar words with your child.

Linda Coates Cert Ed, MA.

Sleeping Beauty

retold by Brenda Apsley

illustrated by Gill Guile

Published in Great Britain by World International Publishing Limited,
An Egmont Company, Egmont House, P.O. Box 111, Great Ducie Street, Manchester M60 3BL
Printed in Italy. SBN 7235 8764 7

In a far-off-land lived a king and queen. When their baby daughter was born they were very happy and made plans for a great party to celebrate her birth.

The king and queen sent invitations to all the fairies in the kingdom, but they forgot to ask one very old fairy. She lived in a remote cottage, and no one had seen her for years.

The party was held in the great hall of the royal palace, and all the fairies gathered around the cradle to look at the new royal princess.

One by one the fairies gave their gifts to the baby. One said that she would sing sweetly, one that she would be kind, and another that she would have a tender, loving heart.

As the last of the fairies was about to give the princess her gift, the great doors opened and the very old fairy walked in. She was very angry that she had not been invited.

The old fairy went to the cradle. "Here is my gift for your daughter," she said to the king and queen. "When she is sixteen she will prick her finger on a spindle and die!"

The king and queen begged the old fairy to take back her evil spell, but she would not. "No one insults me and gets away with it!" she cackled, and hobbled out of the room.

Then the last good fairy spoke. "I think I can help," she said. "The princess will indeed prick her finger on a spindle, but she will not die. Instead, she will sleep for a hundred years."

Next day the king ordered that every spinning wheel in his kingdom should be broken up and burned. "Now the princess will not prick her finger," the king said.

Years passed and the royal princess grew up to be beautiful, kind and loving. In time everyone, even the king and queen, forgot about the old fairy's spell.

On the day before the princess's sixteenth birthday she decided to explore the palace, and walked along corridors and up stairs until she came to a small attic door.

The princess went into a darkened room where a very old woman was sitting at a spinning wheel. "What are you doing?" the princess asked the old woman, who was really the evil fairy in disguise.

“I am spinning, my dear,” said the old woman. The princess had never seen anyone spinning before, and she looked closely. “Would you like to try?” asked the old woman.

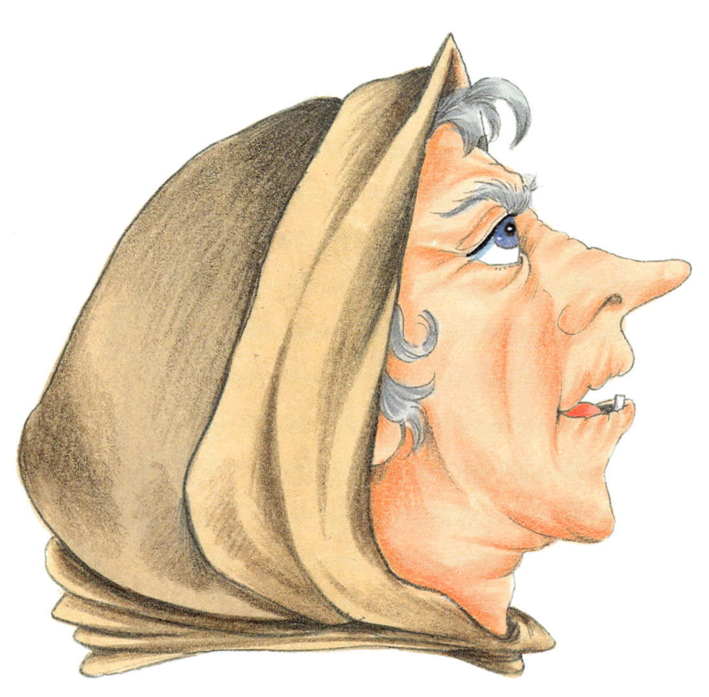

"Yes, please," said the princess. But as soon as she touched the sharp spindle it pricked her finger, drawing a few drops of blood. The evil fairy laughed.

The princess fell to the floor and lay still and lifeless. "That will teach your parents to insult me!" cackled the old fairy, and she hobbled out of the room. Her spell had come true.

When servants found the princess they carried her to her bed. Then the good fairy said, "The princess will sleep for a hundred years, and so will everyone else in the palace."

As she spoke, everyone fell asleep: the king and queen on their thrones, the cooks and maids in the kitchens, and the soldiers on guard duty. Even the cats and dogs slept.

The good fairy waved her wand again and cast a spell on the palace itself. A thick hedge of thorns and brambles grew up around it until it was almost hidden from view.

One hundred years passed and still the palace slept. One day, a young prince rode by and saw the tip of a tower through the thick hedge. He asked a woodcutter what it was.

"They say a royal palace lies behind the hedge," said the woodcutter. "A wicked fairy cast a spell and the princess and her family have slept there for a hundred years."

The prince took out his sword and cut and hacked at the thorny branches. Soon he had cut a narrow path through the bushes, and stood outside the palace gates. He went inside.

Everywhere he looked people and animals were sleeping. He wandered from room to room until he reached the bedroom where the Sleeping Beauty lay.

The princess looked so beautiful that the prince kissed her cheek, and at that moment everyone — including Sleeping Beauty — woke up. Their long sleep was over.

Soon after, the prince and Sleeping Beauty were married. There was a great party. Can you guess who the guest of honour was? Yes — it was the good fairy!